THIS BOOK

BELONGS TO:

Lucy Stewart

Xmas 2018

The *Further* TALE OF PETER RABBIT

THE *Further* TALE OF
PETER RABBIT

BY

Emma Thompson

ILLUSTRATED BY

Eleanor Taylor

FREDERICK WARNE

FOR PETER
CHILDHOOD FRIEND
LEGEND
RABBIT

E.T.

FREDERICK WARNE

Published by the Penguin Group
Penguin Books Ltd, 80 Strand, London WC2R ORL, England
Penguin Group (USA), Inc., 375 Hudson Street, New York, New York 10014, USA
Penguin Group (Canada), 90 Eglinton Avenue East,
Suite 700, Toronto, Ontario, Canada M4P 2Y3
Penguin Ireland, 25 St Stephen's Green, Dublin 2, Ireland
Penguin Group (Australia), 707 Collins Street, Melbourne, Victoria 3008, Australia
Penguin Books India (P) Ltd, 11 Community Centre,
Panchsheel Park, New Delhi 110 017, India
Penguin Group (NZ), 67 Apollo Drive, Rosedale, North Shore 0632, New Zealand
Penguin Books (South Africa) (Pty) Ltd, Block D, Rosebank Office Park, 181 Jan Smuts Avenue,
Parktown North, Gauteng, South Africa 2193

Penguin Books Ltd, Registered Offices: 80 Strand, London WC2R ORL, England

www.peterrabbit.com

First published by Frederick Warne 2012
This edition published by Frederick Warne 2013

001

Original copyright in text and illustrations © Frederick Warne., 2012
Frederick Warne & Co. is the owner of all rights, copyrights and
trademarks in the Beatrix Potter character names and illustrations.
Letter to Mr Rabbit from Emma Thompson copyright © Emma Thompson, 2013
Image of elephant that appears on Emma Thompson's letter reproduced courtesy of Axel Scheffler

Printed and bound in China

Dear Reader,

O N A HOT (ISH) DAY IN SCOTLAND, during what many persisted in calling the 'summer' of 2010, I received a package from an old childhood acquaintance. Surprisingly fresh in my memory, I knew him to be wise yet rash, funny yet dignified and always up to something.

His two most remarkable qualities were that he was 110 years old and a rabbit. The parcel contained some half-eaten radish-tops and a letter inviting me to write a new tale.

He observed in his missive that I was 'a tad naughty', even 'mischievous' – neither of which rang any bells with me or my family (who know me to be a sober, quiet individual who shies away from attention).

Nonetheless it was an invitation I could no more refuse than I could refuse to breathe.

The following pages contain the fruit of that damp season's labour and I wish you the same joy in reading them as I took in writing them.

- E. T.

I HAVE NOT SEEN many rabbits moping, but when they do, their ears droop.

PETER RABBIT was in low spirits. It had been a rainy summer, his blue coat had been torn by briars and his shoes were hurting.

"What I need," he said, "is a change of scene."

Benjamin Bunny advised against it. "Too many carts on the road," he said. "Too many owls, and too many foxes."

DISCOURAGED, Peter squeezed under the gate into Mr. McGregor's garden, intending to steal a lettuce.

What should he find by the greenhouse but an interesting basket smelling of onions?

He opened it and climbed in.

INSIDE, wrapped in brown paper, were some excellent sandwiches of cheese and pickle.

He ate them all.

It was cosy in the basket so he fell asleep.

13

WHEN he woke up the basket was *joggling*. Fearfully, Peter lifted the lid and peeked out.

The basket was in a cart and the cart was on the open road!

Badly frightened, and with no idea of what to do, Peter shot under the neatly folded blanket on the bottom.

THE joggling went on for a
very
very
very
Long Time.

17

WHEN it stopped, someone lifted the lid of the basket.

"Who's eaten our picnic?" screeched Mrs. McGregor, twitching away the blanket.

"THIEF!!" she screamed.

Peter bolted just in time.

HE ran until he could run no more. Panting at the foot of a tall pine-tree, he looked about. A stream ran clear over mossy grey stones, harebells bobbing at the rim.

The call of a buzzard made him look up in fright to see high purple hills. Peter, who had a sore paw from running, limped out and stared. He had left his shoes in the basket.

"AYE," said a deep voice, "no matter where we've been or where we're going, 'tis the hills draw us back."

Peter turned to see a HUGE black rabbit in a kilt, a dagger thrust into the top of his laced-up boot.

"Ye'll be Peter Rabbit," said the giant. Peter nodded.

"Finlay McBurney at your service. News of your disappearance came up with the mail-coach. Your mother's fit to be tied. Follow me."

Peter followed. He thought it better not to mention the sandwich-basket.

THE Scottish burrow was hung
with bunches of bog-cotton.

The peat on the fire smelt sharp.
Mrs. McBurney, her ears tied
in a neat knot, met Peter with a
bowl of steaming porridge.

HE was put to bed with much kindness, on a sack filled with sheepswool and heather.

WHEN he woke, Mrs. McBurney had made potato scones for his breakfast.

"Hurry now dearie," she said.

"Today's the Big Day! Finlay's defending his title!"

"Oh, good," said Peter, not wishing to appear ignorant – even though he had no idea what 'defending his title' meant.

IN a clearing not far from the burrow, rabbits from all the different clans were gathering.

At last, Finlay appeared holding up a great golden cup. "I challenge all comers!" he bellowed.

Peter thought it was very exciting.

THE Games began.

Most of them involved throwing something heavy as far as possible. Finlay won nearly all of them.

Quite soon, Peter thought it very boring.

To the side, the bracken was flattened into a path, which Peter followed, cautiously.

He came upon a sign, which read "KEEP OUT".

I imagine it will not surprise you to hear that Peter
            did not
                KEEP OUT.

He WENT IN.

THERE, protected by willow-fencing, lay an *unusually* large RADISH.

It must have measured three rabbits round! It also smelt delicious and Peter was very hungry.

He thought no-one would notice if he took a little nibble off the end.

Accordingly, he scratched his way under the willow-fence and took a bite.
And then,
another.
And another.

By the time Peter had stopped eating, he was INSIDE the radish.

Feeling cosy, he fell asleep.

When he woke up, the radish
was
joggling.

"Not again," thought Peter.

ALL of a sudden, the radish was tipped up and Peter tumbled out.

HE found himself back in the clearing. All the rabbits were shouting "Throw the radish! Throw the radish!"

"Young cousin Peter!" boomed Finlay. "Be a good wee bunny and toss me yon radish!"

This was unfair.

Finlay knew the radish was far too heavy for a little rabbit to throw all by himself. But he did not know that most of the radish was *inside* Peter.

PETER picked the radish up by its top-knot. Everyone laughed at him.

Peter whirled the radish around his head and let go.

It flew clean over Finlay and landed with a thud on the other side of the clearing.

Everyone stopped laughing.

THEN a rabbit in a tam o'shanter yelled, "Peter Rabbit wins the Cup!"

Peter was raised aloft on dozens of rough paws and bounced about until he felt sick.

I am sorry to say that he had eaten far too much radish.

WHEN they put him down, Finlay came up with the Cup. "Aye, ye've won fair and square, laddie!" he said. "The Cup is yours!"

Peter felt awful.

"I didn't win it fair and square!" he exclaimed.

He told Finlay the truth about the hollow radish. When he'd finished, there was a *long* silence.

FINALLY, Finlay threw back his ears and roared with laughter.

Finlay kept his Golden Cup and Peter's clever trick became the greatest story in the history of the Games.

THEY all feasted on young turnips and the remains of the radish.

Everyone was *very* cheerful, but Peter was homesick.

THE very next day, Finlay hid him behind a sack of letters on the mail-coach south. Mrs. McBurney had mended his blue jacket and given him a fat little haggis for his mother.

"Haste ye back, wee Cousin Peter," said Finlay. Then he coughed and turned away. Something seemed to have got into his eye.

Peter thought it was a midge.

THERE was great rejoicing in the sand-bank when Peter arrived home. His mother had worn herself to a *frazzle* in his absence.

She did not mention the shoes.

PETER was made to tell the story of the giant radish again and again. Benjamin Bunny always paid it particular attention.

One morning, as the first leaves were turning, he crept up beside Peter.

"Um . . . next time you need a change of scene," he said. "Can I come?"

THE END

It all started with a letter . . .

PETER RABBIT came to life in a picture letter by Beatrix Potter in 1893, written to cheer up a poorly boy called Noel Moore. In this letter you can see many of the words and pictures that went on to become *The Tale of Peter Rabbit*: naughty Peter ignores Mrs. Rabbit's instruction to stay away from Mr. McGregor's garden, and so his very first adventure begins.

Eastwood Dunkeld
Sep 4th 93

My dear Noel,
I don't know what to write to you, so I shall tell you a story about four little rabbits. whose names were —

Flopsy, Mopsy, Cottontail

and Peter

In fact, many of Beatrix Potter's original tales began as picture letters – a tradition that we have continued all these years later.

FOR THE ATTENTION OF:
Ms. Emma Thompson
London

To celebrate 110 years since the publication of *The Tale of Peter Rabbit*, Frederick Warne thought Peter would enjoy setting off on a brand new adventure. But who to dream up such a tale? The exceptionally talented and slightly mischievous Emma Thompson seemed the perfect choice.

Not long after this important decision was made, Peter Rabbit himself composed a letter to Emma, and so began an enchanting correspondence culminating in the tale you have just read. Over the page you can read the original letter from Peter to Emma, and her response, so that you can see how this wonderful new story began.

Ms. Emma Thompson
London

Honoured Madam,

I write to ask whether you
have heard of me? I do hope
so as I am almost 110 years old.

Miss Beatrix Potter was
a big fan of mine and
wrote a whole
story about me.

I am curious to find out
if you would be interested
in writing the next story
about **ME**. It has come to my
attention that you are a writer of
distinction but a tad naughty and
I have noticed a certain mischievous

twinkle in your eye — which leads me to think we will get on uncommonly well. It would be a great honour if you were to agree to this, I should so like to be in another story.

Before you make your decision, there are some things you should know about me. Although I'm 110 years old in 2012, I'm still very agile; that cranky old farmer, Mr. McGregor hasn't caught me yet.

Some people seek to malign my character and refer to me as naughty, but you can't blame a rabbit for wanting to have some fun. Most importantly, I'm partial to radishes (I do hope you enjoy the ones I am sending you).

Oops! Sorry!

I'm afraid I got rather hungry...

My cousin Benjamin
has just informed me
that the spring cabbages
in Mr. McGregor's garden look very
tasty today, so I must hop off now.
Lippity – l'ippity. I wonder what
new adventures await us?

Kindly reply by return.

Yrs. truly,

Peter Rabbit

P.S. Do you own a py-dish?

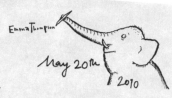

Emma Thompson

May 20th 2010

Dear Mr Rabbit —

in receipt of your extraordinary proposal, may I first say how unusual it is and what an honour it is to be thus addressed by — and your natural modesty will rebel at the epithet but it is nonetheless justified — a Legend.

I am, of course, conversant with your story — and with the great genius of the person who told it. Needless to say, it is head-swelling to an almost dangerous extent that you should think of me in the same breath. I need to know what you have in mind. You say you are now 110. Are we to proceed, therefore, with a story that reflects the processes and — occasionally unhappy — demands of middle - to - late old age?

Emma Thompson

OR is it to your youthful memories
that I should direct my imagination?
My style, I should hasten to tell you,
is different to Miss Potter's. I would
not dare to emulate nor attempt to
repeat the absolute perfection she wrought
with both pen and paint.
Rather, I would — after sitting over
a pipe or two of rabbit tobacco —
attempt a new prose worthy of your
status and if you will be good enough
to advise me, a story that will
grow with you into the future —
as you have grown before.
Dear Mr Rabbit, I cannot, indeed,
cannot thank you enough for your
kindest offer — I await your
response with eagerness.

Emma Thompson

Ever your faithful
servant —

Mrs E. Thompson

P.S. I meant to send a
chocolate but something seems
to have happened to it...

P.P.S. please excuse the writing-paper.
I must assure you it indicates
no preference of elephant over
rabbit. No preference at all.